I0760734

BY MARIA CAIAZZA

MODERN TALES OF OLD SERIES

Heartless
The Seven Ravens

MODERN TALES OF OLD

THE SEVEN RAVENS

MODERN TALES OF OLD

THE

SEVEN RAVENS

MARIA CAIAZZA

This novel's story and characters are a work of fiction. Any resemblance to actual persons, places, or events is purely coincidental. Certain long-standing public offices are mentioned, but the characters and situations involved are wholly imaginary.

ISBN:
9781957257136 (ebook)
9781957257143 (paperback)
9781957257150 (hardcover)

For the people who are no longer with us to read this.

PROLOGUE

PEOPLE ALWAYS UNDERESTIMATED Heidi, and she liked it that way. Playing the meek, naïve, foolish girl in the public eye suited her just fine. It meant she could walk around her family's residence without raising suspicion, which often paid off in spades. Today was no exception as she eavesdropped on two maids talking about her in hushed tones in an area they thought was private.

"What about the young miss?" Ada, the younger of the two, said in a mousy voice.

"It's like I said. She's a sweet girl, but shame on their father for making her brothers pay the price for her to live," an older woman named Greta responded.

A pregnant pause fell between them as they worked.

"I don't understand what you're talking about. The young miss has no siblings."

"Don't you?"

There must've been some sort of unspoken or hushed conversation on the other side of the door. Heidi imagined hand gestures shared between the two women. Perhaps, Greta drew her thumb across her neck to inform Ada of someone's untimely demise. She'd never know.

"You must think I'm a fool, Greta," Ada said in hushed tones. "The master wouldn't hurt a fly."

"He can, and he did. You aren't old enough to remember. I was there. I saw it. Her brothers left; he cursed them, and they never returned. Be careful, my dear. Please? For me?"

Ada scoffed.

The pair must've exchanged another unspoken conversation. Heidi could only make guesses about the interaction, but moments later, a sense overtook her; one of those feelings that came with no perceptible input. She didn't know where the urge came from, but she followed her instincts. They never steered her wrong before. Every time she ignored her intuition, she regretted it. Even though she wanted to hear the rest of the conversation, she pulled away from her hiding place.

With silent steps, she strode away, her mind reeling.

Was there truth to what she overheard? All her life, she thought she was an only child, but Greta said otherwise. She knew the woman liked to exaggerate, but how much of the tale got blown out of proportions? Furthermore, how much could she take at face value?

A sigh escaped her. She wrung her hands.

Sometimes, she hated spying on people. Now, she had a mystery to solve without so much as a lead to send her towards the next clue. Where should she look for more information about her supposed brothers without arousing the suspicions of either her parents or their staff?

Pretending to be an airheaded nitwit to the average onlooker took more work than she cared to admit.

As she passed the sitting room, an idea struck her. Seeing the books lining the walls gave her a brilliant idea. She would research her family history and lineage. If they asked, she'd tell her parents she took an interest in the past since her choices shaped their family's future. Isn't that what they said about history repeating itself?

One side of her lips curled upward.

It was so easy to read people and lead them to believe whatever she wanted. After she armed herself with more information, she'd confront her parents and find out the truth. For now, she'd lie in wait while conducting research. Yes, she needed more information before doing anything too rash.

ONE

AFTER RESEARCHING THE PRECIOUS little information she could find regarding her so-called brothers, Heidi felt less than prepared for a conversation about them. Somebody went to great effort redacting them from any documents she could get her hands on at home, but they couldn't destroy publicly available information from the internet.

Part of her wanted to drop the subject and move on with her life. Curiosity got the better of her, though. She couldn't pretend they didn't exist any longer. Her thirst for knowledge was insatiable. She needed to know what happened to them, to understand *why* they disappeared.

Her mind wouldn't let her rest until she knew.

With shoulders squared and head held high, she walked into the dining room and took her seat. She sat across from her mother while her father took the head of the table. Despite her growing impatience to start the conversation she desired, she remembered her manners. *Barely*. A butler placed their meals at the table, and they began their evening ritual.

Her father talked about business and asked her mother about the goings on at the residence. Only then did he even deign to look at his only daughter. After finding out about her long-lost siblings, Heidi wondered if he treated them the same, or if their absence created this loving yet distant version of their father. She wondered whether she got the better or worst side of the bargain. If her parents had children before her, did they coddle and dote on them, or were they restrictive and firm? The biggest complaint she had about the siblings she never knew were all the what-ifs. Her parents needed to clear some things up before she went mad.

What was the point in agonizing over the possibilities before she knew if Greta's words were true? She had to stop doing this to herself. Talking to herself in these topsy-turvy circles solved nothing.

"Heidi?" a bodiless voice asked, snapping her out of her reverie.

After several beats, Heidi blinked and shook her head. She regained focus and realized her father tried speaking to her while her thoughts spiraled.

"Oh. I- I'm so sorry, father. I'm afraid I missed your question. My attention was elsewhere."

A blush colored her freckled cheeks.

His full-bodied laugh shook his body and filled the room with its levity. "You need to come down from the clouds, my sweet."

Hearing his words didn't reassure her at all. In fact, it summoned images of men who looked similar to her wearing white robes with wings and a halo. She fought to school her expression, but despite herself, she knew her true feelings shone through. It irked her to show weakness, even for a moment. As a future female business owner, she couldn't let others in the male dominated industry see her as weak. Her father made her practice her best disinterested look often.

Realizing her father still expected an answer, she cleared her throat.

"Sorry about my distraction, father. I didn't intend any disrespect. If you were asking about my after school lessons, I didn't attend them again. Please forgive me; I know you pay my tutors well. There's a nasty rumor circulating through the manor's staff. I've spent my time researching everything I can without neglecting my responsibilities too much."

Heidi's father stared at her, dumbfounded. She could almost hear his internal dialogue. He usually saw her as a demure little thing who never stepped a toe out of line, but she outright disobeyed his wishes about missing her lessons again today. Then, she started their evening meal with an impassioned speech about the rumor mill at their residence. It came as no surprise that the fork in his hand remained in a tenuous hold between his fingers. If he dropped it, the clattering noise would sound like a bomb going off in the otherwise silent dining area.

A few beats passed, and he said, "Well then, why don't you tell me about this *rumor* you discovered before I pass judgment on your poor life choices," through gritted teeth.

His attitude didn't surprise her. Honestly, she'd expected worse after lying to him about feeling unwell when she skipped her lessons earlier in the week. If he punished her without hearing her out, it still wouldn't shock her.

"Well, I was walking down the hall when I heard a couple of maids discussing me. It surprised me, so I stopped, of course. I wanted to hear what they had to say. Yes, I know eavesdropping is rude, but they *were* speaking about me. If somebody is talking about me behind my back, I feel like I should know these things in order to make changes where necessary.

"As I listened, they discussed my siblings. *Brothers*, they said. Until today, I didn't know I had siblings, let alone multiple. As soon as I heard, I took to our private library and scoured the books about our family lineage, trying to find anything we had concerning them. Our records leave something to be desired, unless you hid the documents they're in for whatever reason. It made me think you were ashamed of them."

Across the table, Heidi's mother broke her silence with a long, loud sigh. She lifted her knife, and for a moment, Heidi thought she intended to cut the tension in the room rather than her pork chop.

When she spoke, her tone was clipped. "You should've told her about this ages ago, but it's better late than never, Christoph."

Heidi gulped; she hoped they didn't hear the nervous tick. Clearly, this was a touchy subject. Based on body language alone, the entire room was tense. On top of that, her mother never used her father's full name unless she meant business.

"Don't be like that, Anneliese. You know I didn't do it on purpose. I've apologized a thousand times-"

"Then, you'll only need to say it a thousand and one more," she cut him off. "The curse was unforgivable. They were *children*. Have some grace and own up to your mistakes for once in your life."

The more Heidi's mother spoke, the more red her father turned. As he neared on a vibrant puce color, Heidi thought he would burst.

"It wasn't like that! You were there." The wild desperation in his voice made it crack with raw emotion. It looked like his eyes might bug right out of his head if he stared at her with any more intensity. His arms moved over the table towards Anneliese. The hands curled into claws like he wanted to grab and shake her.

Heidi coughed to distract her father or somehow diffuse the situation without confrontation. She didn't realize how touchy this subject was for them. A wave of guilt washed over her. She loved it when she caused marital drama between her parents. Not. She hated it, and in her opinion, anybody who took joy in watching the suffering of others was either a psychopath or trying to sell you something.

Heidi waited for one of them to speak, but when neither of them jumped in, she said, "Why don't you start from the beginning for the ignorant among the group?"

Her mother didn't hesitate. "I think that's a splendid idea, sweetheart. Why don't you explain what happened, Christoph."

He muttered several oaths under his breath about girl power and ganging up on him. His shoulders slumped. He probably wondered when he lost control over this situation? He drew himself up and took a sip of water.

"Very well, Anna. You're right. Though you could stand to be nicer to me. I'm an old man for God's sake! My heart can't take it."

"I was at your annual physical. Your doctor says you're as healthy as a horse."

"I think we're getting off topic here."

Anneliese schooled a smirk, which Heidi caught. Her mother loved it when she took charge.

Christoph looked between them in obvious defeat. A deep sigh escaped him. He deflated further as he considered how to explain things in a way his daughter might understand.

"Heidi, the joy your mother and I felt on the day you were born is beyond anything I could explain. After seven boys, you, my sweet, were the first girl. You're a precious, beautiful treasure who shines brighter than any of the wares I sell. But you were small and weak. The midwives didn't think you'd make it through the day, so I sent your brothers to get blessed water for your baptism in a rush.

"There were seven of them. I didn't think such a simple task would take so long. I thought they'd gotten distracted and started to play instead of running the errand. They couldn't mess things up and forget to bring the water we asked for. You were more important than anything to me then, and you still are. I only want the best for you. That's when I stepped outside to look for them with growing frustration in my heart.

"I couldn't find them right away. So, I cursed and wished they'd become ravens so they could fly back home faster. I don't know what happened. Maybe somebody magical overheard, or perhaps, I possess a magic I don't know how to use. Regardless-"

He gulped down thick saliva, much the same as his daughter. The sound filled the room with his palpable anxiety.

Several beats passed. Heidi adjusted herself in her seat to break some of the tension.

"A group of seven ravens flew overhead less than a minute after I spoke the words. And- and-" he trailed off.

Christoph covered his eyes. His hands fisted his hair as he devolved into sobs. The visible parts of his face turned an unattractive burgundy color.

Her father didn't look capable of explaining the last part of the story, so she turned her attention to her mother, who placed a hand on his shoulder and rubbed soothing circles there.

"We never saw the boys again. We believe they were the ravens Chris saw. They didn't return home, which is something we'll never understand since we wanted to remove the spell. Your father thinks they're angry at him for doing it, but we'll never know for certain. You see, the men in our family are an obstinate, unforgiving bunch-"

"Hey!" Heidi's father glowered.

"Oh, shut it. I love you despite your flaws. You know I wouldn't change a thing about you for the world. Now, where was I?" she asked rhetorically.

Heidi giggled at the interaction between them. It was good to see how in love they were after all their years together.

"We were so distraught by losing your brothers and surprised you made it through that you went without a name for a whole week before we decided on Heidi."

Once she heard everything, she wanted to process things on her own. "If you don't mind, I'd like to excuse myself. After such an eventful evening, I'd like to get some rest."

"Of course, my sweet," Christoph said. He waved a hand to dismiss her. "Enjoy your evening."

She gave them both a respectful dip of the head and shuffled away. Before she made it out of the room, she came to a halt. The decisiveness with which she stopped made her parents look up to regard her again, despite their earlier dismissal. "If you don't mind?"

"What is it, dear?" her mother asked.

"It was Greta I overheard talking about my brothers. Call it petty, but if we can't trust her to keep quiet about something so important and embarrassing to our family, perhaps it's best she not stay here long enough to share any more sensitive information."

Heidi's words hung like a noose in the air between them.

"I'll take it under consideration," her father said after a moment's hesitation.

She nodded again and didn't bother to respond. Heidi knew a dismissal when she heard one. If she ran the place, Greta wouldn't work for them come tomorrow, but nobody respected a teenager's opinions. Most of the time, she liked it that way. People could think what they liked about her. The more unassuming they thought she was, the better chance she stood at manipulating and lying her way into getting what she wanted. Being underestimated came with its benefits and pitfalls, but the good outweighed the bad by a country mile. She could use people's perception of her to get her way in the future, especially when she took over the family business.

When she made it to her room, she closed the door behind her with a click and took a seat on her bed where she toed off her shoes. She flexed and pointed her feet. The stretch felt good. She wanted to take a walk, but she wanted to be inside to hear the hubbub when the yelling started. Watching the drama unfold was fun.

The bright, blue skies outside drew her attention to the window. She imagined seven ravens flying by, but there was nothing there when she blinked. As she stared at the outside world, she saw everything and nothing. Her attention and thoughts were unfocused as she processed her next moves. If she remained here, nothing changed. She'd take over for her father's business one day, probably marry another affluent merchant or perhaps a minor noble. Her family's power and influence promised her a good life. She couldn't imagine anything else.

But.

There was always a but.

Now that she knew her brothers existed, she would always wonder if her parents wanted her to run the family business because of her merits or because they had no other choice. It would hurt her to know they'd chosen her by default rather than earning their trust and respect.

She sighed so heavily, it sounded like she was a deflating balloon in the otherwise silent room. Damn it all. Until today, her life was perfect. She grew up in a happy home. Her life was comfortable, loving, and simple. As an only child, she didn't need to fight for her inheritance. Unless she screwed up something beyond repair, she'd get what she deserved. After years of training, she was close to having it all. She'd go to college and get her MBA. Then, her father could retire and hand over the reins of the business to her.

However, her entire perspective on her life changed today. She knew a male child would traditionally take precedence over her in the family business, but since she knew more than them, she could prove her worth over the boys. Taking the prize without so much as a fight sounded like a hollow victory.

Heidi groaned and waved a hand to clear her head of the spiraling thoughts. Now, she was thinking in circles. She needed to stay logical about this, and it all came down to one question.

Could she live with allowing the current line of succession to follow its natural course, or did she want to fight for glory and prove herself? How did she already know her answer?

It was crazy to give up the easy road. Still, she wanted to do it.

Sometimes, decisiveness came as a blessing and a curse.

"Dammit," she said to herself.

She placed her face in her hands and groaned, "Why me?"

TWO

DESPITE THE VOICE INSIDE HER HEAD urging her to pack fast and leave even more quickly, a nagging feeling told Heidi to take her time. So, of course, she listened. Why change a winning strategy now? She didn't have time for regret, mistakes, or anything else. When intuition screamed for her to come, she followed. She believed human intuition was its own powerful magic, mundane as it may be. That's why she kept her walls up and avoided trusting certain people; when they revealed their true colors, she registered little surprise. Call it cynical, but she knew where she stood. Her senses knew better than her, and she trusted them.

Instead of packing in a flurry, she took her time and thought through each garment, toiletry, and first aid supply she packed. Instead of dealing with an overflowing backpack she needed to lighten, she chose luxury items to make the journey easier. First on her list, she wound up her phone charger and slid it into the front pocket, gingerly patting the outside when she finished. She would rather die than let her phone get below twenty percent. Who didn't feel the same nowadays? Her cell phone was her lifeline. With the power of technology, one phone call meant safety as long as she had cell service.

By the time she came to the end of her mental list, she placed a sheathed knife at the top of the bag. Most of the time, she used the thing to open plastic wrap or boxes she received in the mail, but out in the real world? A knife was multi-functional with personal protection being the foremost in her mind. Fighting didn't come naturally to her, but having something to help if needed eased her nerves.

Finished packing with some room to spare, she puzzled over what else to add. One of her hands gripped her chin with the juncture of her thumb and pointer finger. The index finger tapped her cheek a couple times before she sprung into action. How silly; she'd almost forgotten food.

Using light footsteps, she made her way towards the kitchen. Having lived here her entire life, she knew where each squeaky floorboard lay in her path, and she strafed around them with deft precision.

It took an effort to keep a swell of pride at bay. Her plan came together with ease. In no time, she'd run away with no one the wiser. Nobody would think to stop her until it was too late. Confidence and control felt good. Plenty of other girls her age, and some even older, never felt this way. Her strategies were without equal. Once she retrieved her brothers, she'd prove her worth to her parents without a doubt. She was the best of the Schneider siblings without a doubt.

As she rounded the corner into the kitchen, she came to a halt and slunk back into shadow. Arrogance almost became her undoing. In her defense, she didn't expect to find her father and Greta sharing a one-sided conversation in the kitchen. When her father got angry, he usually raised his voice. It sent a shiver down her spine to hear him speaking so quietly now. Even though her gut told her to retreat, she ignored it this time. She needed to know what was happening. Her curiosity begged to know more before she even processed a single word spoken between the pair.

"I paid you for your silence, woman," Christoph said between gritted teeth, enunciating each syllable with explosive consonants. His knuckles cracked when he balled his fists. The loud pops filled the room.

Heidi imagined spittle spewing out of his mouth as he enunciated each word. She'd heard him angry before. In fact, she'd been on the receiving end of his ire on more than one occasion, but she'd never witnessed anything like this. Until now, she never considered her father capable of rage like this. Lucky thing he loved her. The servant didn't stand a chance.

"I didn't mean no harm by it, sir," Greta said in a monotone, which contrasted how she sounded when speaking to Ada days before.

Heidi's eyebrows raised up into her hairline. Either Greta faced men with a temper regularly, or she had no sense of self preservation. The next beat, Heidi's face screwed up as she pondered the old woman's meaning. Her memory and Greta's memory of the conversation she overheard were different.

"If you intended no harm, you never would've brought it up!" Christoph whispered despite his seething anger. His breath grew more labored with each passing second. "Spewing your frivolous gossip causes nothing but grief to me and my family."

From her hiding place, she could envision her father's face turning candy apple red. Her father would have a coronary if he didn't learn to control his anger. She wished he would speak louder rather than bottle up all of his irritation. He was hard to hear like this. Then again, if he raised his voice, she could've overheard the conversation from her room.

Several beats of silence passed as Greta considered how to best respond. "I'm sorry, sir. It won't happen again."

"You're right, it won't. Get out of here. You're fired."

Heidi moved her hand to cover her mouth to suppress the sound of her inhaled breath. She knew her father's temper often got the best of him, but even though she asked for this, she didn't expect him to follow through on the suggestion. After the initial surprise waned, a thrill rushed through her. Did this mean he trusted her judgment on important matters such as staffing?

It felt unreal, but she allowed herself a moment of silence to bask in the feeling. For a second, she considered giving up on her newfound mission. This validation would carry her forward into the future, but the dark shadow of her raven-ous brothers lurked like the monster under a child's bed, ready to spring up and crush her at the first opportunity. No. She couldn't allow the possibility to come to pass. Trust wasn't something she came by easily, and her parents rarely did anything to earn it. Fate couldn't intervene here; she needed to create her own destiny.

Heidi's hand lowered from her mouth. She released a heavy breath of air as the tension in her muscles uncoiled and relaxed. She realized she'd lost track of the conversation in the kitchen. The pair were uncomfortably quiet, sharing pointed jabs at each other back and forth under their breaths. She rolled her eyes and considered going back to her room to pass the time, but before she could escape, Greta stalked by. The older woman's chestnut colored eyes felt like they pierced into her soul as she glared.

The urge to shiver hit her like a sack of potatoes, but she reined in her reaction. She learned to control and hone her instincts during her tutoring sessions. Among people her age, she stood head and shoulders above the rest. Against an irate servant, she could hold her own during a staring contest.

Still, the way Greta looked at her almost caused her physical pain. If the woman could cut her down using nothing more than the power of her mind and force of will, Heidi knew she'd already be dead. Damn.

Double damn.

Apparently, she still needed to learn quite a bit more to achieve Greta's level of skill. Once the servant disappeared down the hall, Heidi slumped down to the floor. She wrapped her arms around her legs and pulled her knees up into her chest as she fought to calm down. Greta impressed her. Well, she was equal parts impressed, exhausted, and terrified. She didn't expect the strength and suddenness of the encounter, and now, she couldn't keep it from living in her head without paying rent! The audacity.

She harrumphed and stood back up to her full height, squaring her shoulders. Nobody could make her feel less-than, especially not an unemployed gossip monger.

Leaning as close to the entrance to the kitchen as she dared, she closed her eyes and listened. Not a peep came for several seconds. Either her father calmed down in record time, or he already took his leave. She already knew the answer without so much as stealing a glance. Whirling around the corner, she sprung into action, packing non-perishable items in quart and gallon-sized resealable bags to keep them from spilling if accidentally opened. Nothing was worse than sticky, ruined clothes inside of a suitcase or backpack. She shuddered. The sensory visual of a soggy scarf under her fingertips did not cause joy.

After she got everything packaged, she neatly tucked it all into a canvas bag and slung it over her shoulder. With her bag packed and plenty of provisions, she only had one thing left to do. She twisted the knob on her bedroom door and closed it slowly. Nobody was around to hear the tiny sound it made when it slid into place. She placed the bag inside of her backpack and tucked it in snugly. As she fiddled with the zippers, she took care to tuck and fold things inside to force it closed. How could she go from underpacking to over packing so easily? She shook her head at the irony of the situation. It was just like her to hit both sides of the spectrum somehow; she was her parents' child after all.

Once it closed, she fell back onto her bed and stared up at the ceiling for a moment. Staring at the popcorn until she could see pictures in the texture was an oddly mesmerizing pass time. She knew she was procrastinating, delaying the inevitable, but when she thought this might be the last time she lay on her own bed for a long time, she wanted to steal away a few extra moments.

"What is it you're waiting for, Heidi, permission? You won't get it. May as well get on with it," she said before shoving herself up into a sitting position and grabbing her backpack. The strap strained against the weight of the pack. It was so cumbersome that it threw her off balance. She knew compensating for the heavy load would leave her back and shoulders aching before the end of the evening.

"No regrets, girl. You've got this."

Heidi moved to leave her room with a couple decisive strides towards her door before hesitating. Instead of leaving, she pivoted to her desk, where she yanked a piece of lined paper out of a notebook. She grabbed the first pen she found, which was a purple clicky one. With the press of her thumb, she started her draft.

For a second, she imagined a grand and elaborate letter, explaining all the ins and outs of her plans and reasoning. As much as she'd love to let her family know about the infinitesimal details, she decided less was more. One of her favorite teachers taught her the acronym K.I.S.S. This seemed like a suitable moment to use it.

"Keep it simple, stupid," she muttered as she wrote two sentences to get her point across. With a satisfied nod and a flourish, she signed the bottom of her note.

I've left to rescue my brothers. Don't worry too much about me. I'll be back soon.

Love,

Heidi

"Good enough."

Now, she could leave. She marched out of her bedroom and towards the kitchen. Nobody should be down there at this time of night. It would make her escape that much easier. Then, she hesitated once again.

She forgot something. The item wasn't necessary, per se, but it would help with quality of life when she came to the end of her adventure. When she thought about meeting her brothers logically, they never knew her. She was an infant when they disappeared, so evidence of her identity may prove helpful. Her fingers moved up to her forehead, and she rubbed her temples. Stealing her father's signet ring sounded like a recipe for disaster. What other choice did she have?

Closing her eyes, she pondered her options. If she left without the item, how else would they know her? Would they believe her story or call her a liar? If somebody came to her with a similar wild story, she'd ignore them outright. Her head gave a quick, jerking shake. She couldn't afford to go to the trouble of finding them only for them to turn her away at the last minute. She needed this.

With a grunt, she placed her pack down. She rolled her shoulders, and one hand massaged an aching shoulder. Hopefully, she'd get stronger given some time. Otherwise, this little adventure wouldn't prove fun.

Heidi waited until a couple hours after her parents retired for the evening. Under the cover of night, she crept down the hallway and to the door of their room. She knelt there and pressed her ear to a cupped hand against the door. No sound came through. She hoped this meant they were deeply asleep by now. With no sliver of light visible from the other side, she tried her luck.

One hand reached up at a painfully slow pace and turned the knob until she felt it disengage. Now, she just needed to open it. Her whole body tensed, coiled tight and ready to run at the first sign of trouble. If one of her parents caught her, she couldn't lie her way out of this mess. It'd been years since she last woke them from a bad dream in the middle of the night.

She drew in a ragged breath before pushing the door open, like some portal to another world she didn't know she could survive. Her heart hammered in her chest, threatening to jump out of her body. Somehow, the hinges didn't squeak. Thank the gods.

In the darkness, she squinted towards the bed. Neither of her parents stirred. Her eyes remained glued to them as she crawled on her hands and toes to her father's side table. One hand reached up and patted along the top, scrambling to find the ring. As she moved with increasing speed and frustration, she felt something metallic brush the tips of her fingers. She swiped for it. Her heart skipped a beat when she heard whatever it was clatter down onto the surface. Her jaw clamped tight. She might as well have thrown a hand grenade for all the noise she just made. Her eyes locked onto the bed as she watched and waited. She flinched when her mother sat up, and she crouched to the floor, praying she didn't get caught.

"Buttercup? Is that you?" Anneliese whispered as she searched around the room.

Heidi covered her mouth with a hand, stifling giggles when she realized her mother thought she was the cat. She drew the hand away for a second, and purred, "Prooow."

She watched the silhouette of her mother's shoulders slump at the sound.

"Can it, wretched beast. The rest of us sleep at night while you nap on the windowsill all day."

As her mother rolled over and closed her eyes, Heidi stood up, grabbed her father's signet ring, and crept out the door. That was too close.

Five minutes later, she snuck out the door, and she only planned to return when she could bring her brothers with her.

THREE

EVEN THOUGH HER FAMILY LIVED without the benefit of spell casting in their everyday lives, it didn't mean they didn't reap the benefits of it. Magic made life easier, and she decided to enlist the help of a local witch to start her search. She knew the place well. Children would stop in front of the woman's yard, point at the house, and whisper tall tales, none of which ever proved true. Otherwise, the town would've banished or jailed her ages ago.

Still, children and the internet circulated nasty rumors, regardless of evidence to the contrary. Heidi's class shared a discord channel, and one thread contained days' worth of creepypasta stories about the woman. She was glad the server was private. If adults learned about what the students said about them, they'd ground every child in town for a decade.

Even though it was the middle of the night, the lights inside glowed, illuminating the surrounding yard. The woman sat on her porch, working on some sort of yarn craft. She was middle-aged with dark brown hair, made lighter by strands of the purest silver woven throughout and pulled back into a simple yet elegant bun at the nape of her neck. Despite the whispers about evil witches and black magic, her kind smile and inviting home and garden disarmed Heidi as she approached the gate.

Their eyes met for a long moment of silence. Even though neither spoke a word, an entire conversation passed between the pair by looks alone. Finally, Heidi lifted the latch on the gate and stepped onto the property.

"Welcome to my home," the witch broke the tension, motioning for Heidi to join her inside after she placed her crochet project down.

Heidi nodded, but she hesitated. She felt rooted to the ground just outside of the witch's home. Why did this feel so wrong? She went over the situation again, and instead of going inside, she took a step back. Nobody was awake at this hour, but this *witch* sat on the deck waiting for her to arrive like an honored guest.

"How did you know I was coming?"

The witch laughed. "My specialty is in augury, young lady. If you'd come in and take a seat, I can make you some tea to calm your nerves. I assure you, your parents won't know you've been here for quite some time."

Heidi took several beats to decide whether the witch's laugh sounded sinister. Would she be better off leaving? Was it safe to linger here? What about the stories of witches baking people into pastries and bewitching whole towns?

"Perhaps, I best be going," she said as her eyes darted towards the gate.

"The choice is yours, my dear. Your path is your own, regardless of my place in it."

Part of her wanted to turn away, but Heidi rarely got the opportunity to watch somebody use magic. The mystery of spell casting gave her equal parts the thrill of excitement and ache of fear. If a witch could locate her brothers sixteen years after their disappearance, why couldn't one find them before? What if someone with magic decided the best use of their time was spying on people from an affluent family and selling their secrets as blackmail? She could see so much potential for evil in magic. No wonder so many nasty rumors circulated about people from the magical community. The unknown threats magic posed loomed, waiting to strike the unprepared.

The witch propped the front door open and turned towards a kettle. Every few seconds, she turned her head up to regard Heidi while the young woman thought through her internal argument. An easy smile spread across her features, and she chuckled softly.

"I see much of your father in you," she said. "When he came to me to find your brothers, he did the same."

Her eyebrows jumped into her hairline. She didn't know her parents *tried* to find her brothers. "Why didn't anybody find them if you already gave my parents the information?"

The witch set about making a pot of tea with the deft movements of someone who'd gone about the ritual hundreds or thousands of times over the years.

Even with the woman's back to her, Heidi remained unmoving. Her body felt wooden, and she wondered whether some sort of spell had stricken her. She tested her faculties by flexing her fingers and balling her hands into fists. If the woman bewitched her, she doubted the magic would allow any sort of outward aggression, so she *must* still have control.

"All magic comes at a price," the witch said in a soft, matter-of-fact tone as she added loose tea leaves to a pair of cups. "I told your father as much when he visited sixteen years ago."

The witch glanced back at Heidi. "For brief glances at the future, I sacrifice food, usually scraps of meat. The cost of finding your brothers grows with each passing day. Years ago, I asked your father for you in exchange for my services."

Heidi's foot scraped the ground, but she couldn't bring herself to run away. Why couldn't she leave already? By now, hadn't she seen enough red flags to convince her to get out of here? Instead, a question wrenched itself from her lips so quickly she wondered if she'd thought the words or if the witch spelled them out of her. Perhaps, her instruction in manners and politeness guided her by rote memorization. When she'd met some of her father's professional acquaintances in the past, she'd never experienced this. Was this some sort of omen of luck on her side?

"I apologize for starting off on the wrong foot. My name is Heidi Schneider. It's a pleasure to meet you."

"Caysi Doyle, at your service." The woman gave a respectful nod before turning around.

A moment later, she spun back around with one tea cup in each hand, and a soft, inviting smile in place.

To Heidi, Caysi's footsteps sounded like drums of war, or bombs going off in the distance... And they were getting closer. Still, she remained in her place despite her instincts screaming at her to get out of this place. By some sort of miracle, her fingers clasped onto the proffered tea cup. Her other hand moved underneath it to keep the warm beverage steady. She drew in a breath through her nose, taking in the scent of oranges and cinnamon.

Regardless of her misgivings, her shoulders lowered, and the tightness in her jaw relaxed. Her eyes grew heavy and closed for a second longer than a normal blink. When they reopened, she met the witch's eyes. *No*, she corrected herself. Caysi's eyes. The woman may be a witch, but she had a name. And knowing her name made her much less terrifying. In fact, it humanized her in a way Heidi didn't expect.

She took a tentative step forward regardless of her earlier instincts. When she made it into the space, the pungent and tantalizing aroma of loose leaf tea became stronger. She took a seat at the table, cradling the warm and inviting mug in her hands.

"Thank you," she said as she stared at the cup rather than the other woman. Maybe if she avoided eye contact, she could fend off magic better, or at least, she couldn't see any spells getting slung her way. Ignorance was bliss, after all. Didn't the magical creatures association agree not to use their power on defenseless humans or something? She doubted it meant little more than a hollow promise to those willing to break the law. Just like any other criminal.

"Are you alright?" Caysi asked.

Her voice felt like it came out of nowhere, and Heidi flinched, spilling tea onto the table with the sudden motion. Her cheeks turned bright red as she looked up.

She cleared her throat. "Sorry. Just thinking."

"This must've come as quite the shock." She smiled, sipping her tea. "Your father swore everyone to secrecy after the incident."

"How come you're talking about it then?" Heidi asked, hating how blunt her question sounded. She winced after she finished speaking. So much for tact.

One of the other woman's perfectly groomed eyebrows raised. "Either you weren't listening, or you've already forgotten my specialty. There's no point in hiding anything from somebody who already knows the secret, and you wouldn't be here if you were still in the dark."

She shook her head before meeting the other woman's eyes. "Is Og-whatever some sort of mind reading?"

Caysi didn't hide her chuckle well. "Augury is another word for divination. Through different rites or rituals, I attempt to foretell the future."

"Well, attempting sounds rather definitive." She rolled her eyes.

"The information you learn here is for you to use however you see fit, whether or not you believe it. The question is if you're willing to pay the price or not."

"Name your price, so I can choose whether to pay it already," Heidi clipped, growing impatient.

The witch paused and assessed the young woman for several beats, and Heidi wondered whether the other woman considered her worthy. Her family was well-known as savvy business people. Did Caysi place her in the same high regards as her father, or was her family name nothing more than a label on a disappointing product?

Just as the teenager felt ready to burst with impatience, the older woman drew herself up and said, "The cost of the spell you desire is simple. It requires a life."

"So, you want me to offer you my firstborn child? Isn't this a little too stereotypical fairy tale even for a witch?"

"Magic like mine comes at a price, and since I wouldn't cast this spell for myself, I refuse to make the sacrifice. The offer stands. Are you willing to pay the price to return your brothers home?"

Unlike before, Heidi didn't hesitate. She already knew her answer when she prepared to run away and left her house. Her hand extended, prepared to shake on it.

"Yes," she said with a nod.

Caysi extended a hand and shook on it. "Let's get to work, then."

Heidi quaffed the last of her tea. In the bottom of her cup, she imagined several shapes drawn in the leaves: A knife or, perhaps, an axe? And when she squinted, she saw a rat. Other images came to mind, but she decided not to linger on them. They needed to get to work.

While she was distracted, Caysi bustled out of the room and returned in a whirl of her brightly colored clothes. She laid a world map out on the table and pinned down the edges with their teacups and saucers. From a pocket, she drew a drawstring bag of brightly colored seashells and rocks, which she poured out on the table before them.

"To complete the spell, I'll need a drop of blood from your finger," she said with an outstretched hand. At a second glance, Caysi's other hand offered a needle.

Her hand shook as she extended it to where the other woman held the object. She pricked her finger with the needle and watched the blood pool at the tip of her pinky finger before dropping onto the map in the middle of the ocean somewhere.

"Good, good," the witch said in a soothing and heady voice full of intent.

Neither woman could see it, but they both heard the magic within and without her.

Caysi picked up a handful of the miscellaneous bits from the table and blew a breath into her hands as she held them up. She muttered an indecipherable incantation under her breath and dropped the items onto the map.

FOUR

THANKS TO THE POWER OF MAGIC, HEIDI made her way to the castle at the top of the world. The place became a well-known magical refuge after mysteriously appearing out of thin air about twenty years prior. On her own, she would've wasted time looking elsewhere before deciding to give this place a try.

She arrived around midday and rapped on the massive entry doors. The sound resonated loud and clear to her reckoning, but nobody came to let her in.

Every muscle in her body coiled tight with anticipation. Still, nothing stirred from within. She clicked the lock button on her phone so she could check the time, resolving to wait five excruciating minutes before she potentially made a scene and knocked again.

One.

Two.

Three.

How in the world could it not be five minutes yet? She watched the time tick up once more.

Four.

What was the old adage about a watched pot never boiling? Then again, how would she know five minutes passed unless she *observed* the time?

The remaining few seconds felt like an eternity until the minute *finally* turned over.

Heidi knocked with more vigor, and it felt like the force of her hand hitting the door shook the entire mountain. Nobody could miss it. This time, somebody would come for sure.

She set a timer even though her patience had long since run its course. Several imaginative curses flitted through her mind, but she dared not speak them. A single phrase voiced in her father's frustration caused this mess to begin with. She didn't want to make matters worse.

Several scenarios with increasingly distressing outcomes intruded on her thoughts. Her eyebrows knit together in growing worry until the alarm from her timer startled her. In her surprise, she jumped; the sound literally sprung her into action.

A little, "Eep!" escaped her as she rushed to turn off the phone. The resonant knocking sounds didn't concern her, but the tinkling bell-like sounds of her phone did. Her fingers fumbled for a few seconds, but she soon wrangled the mighty technological beast into submission. Her finger pressed against the screen just right, and she winced. The prick on her finger from Caysi's ritual smarted a little. Luckily, it should heal up soon. It was too small to linger for long.

A huff escaped her as she pocketed her cell phone. When she finished the task, the reality of her situation settled into her very core. She'd politely knocked on the castle doors, clearly indicating her intent to enter. Yet, nobody answered her call. Caysi assured her that she'd find her brothers here. Did the woman lie?

A spark of anger ignited inside of her. She didn't come this far to turn back now. If she went back home with her proverbial tail between her legs, her parents would ground her until the end of her lifetime.

Heidi grabbed the doorknob and yanked as hard as she could, shaking and jiggling it as she used her entire body weight to wrench the thing back.

It didn't budge.

She screamed as she pounded on the door, shouting several colorful expletives she'd learned from her father when they went to business meetings together. In the back of her mind, she could envision the look on her mother's face and the resulting chastisement she'd receive for her word choice, but she didn't care. It couldn't end like this. She bargained away her firstborn with a witch for this information. She *needed* to have something to show for the sacrifice.

With a raw voice and bloodshot eyes, she fell to the ground, sobbing on her hands and knees. The rocky earth dug into her flesh, but she didn't care. Her emotions hurt more.

She was better than this, and she wanted to prove it. As she looked up, an errant ray of sun struck a metallic fixture on the door. The glare of sunlight on metal forced her to squint to get a better look at it. One of her hands moved up to block the light.

When she got closer, she could see the detail the sun illuminated for her.

Just below the doorknob, she found a keyhole. It didn't look like any modern locking mechanism she knew about. Even though this building appeared during modern times, the key must be ancient.

Red hot anger flooded through her. She came all this way without a key. Why didn't the witch tell her?

Heidi didn't know how long it took her to calm down and regain reason, but in her opinion, it was *too* long.

"Okay, think about this logically," she said to herself. She could've thought it out, but putting the words out there into the real world made the plan feel real and tangible. Results felt closer when she turned her thoughts into reality.

"You need a key. An old key. Maybe a magical key. Where can you get one of those?"

No bright ideas came to mind, but she knew with certainty she wouldn't find the key to the castle under the non-existent doormat.

FIVE

HEIDI HIKED DOWN THE TREACHEROUS path out of the mountains where the castle at the end of the world stood. She swore several oaths and grumbled under her breath whenever she came upon a rocky area which required more care to navigate.

The issue her mind kept circling back to was *how* to find a key to such a place. When she thought about it logically, magic created the castle. Therefore, magic must also guard the castle. So, who or what would have a key to this place? And how in the world could *she* find it? She didn't have magic.

"This is hopeless," she said.

"And now you're talking to yourself. Excellent."

When she made it to the bottom of the slope, rocks gave way to an open plain for a while before becoming heavily wooded. As she entered the evergreen forest, she felt a heaviness looming around her that gave her pause. She glanced up, noticing the growing thickness of the branches and boughs overhead. The growing darkness around her must've set her on edge.

Heidi turned her attention away from the canopy to her more immediate surroundings. The area wasn't a clearing per se, but the ground was flat and dry enough for her to use it as a makeshift campsite for the evening.

She tossed her bag onto the ground, and it thunked with the weight. One of her hands moved up to massage the aching muscles in her neck and shoulders. No matter how long this lasted, she couldn't imagine growing used to the physical toll of carrying her overladen pack.

After a few minutes of stretching, she stalked about the area in slow circles, gathering up pieces of tinder she could use to build a fire. Her father took her on a few camping trips growing up, and she felt grateful for what she learned about survival. She couldn't live off the land forever, but roughing it in the woods for a night or two? That, she could manage.

In no time, a fire sparked to life, crackling with heat and light as she sat nearby, propped against a tree for support. Her eyes lingered on the pack she brought. She'd need to build the tent soon, but for now, she needed food and rest.

Her teeth dug into a tough piece of jerky, tearing it apart. The salt lingered on her tongue and made her even more thirsty than before. She stared into the fire, incapable of thought beyond base needs. Food, water, rest.

Long gone were the thoughts of rescuing her siblings. Her eyes closed, and she let them remain lowered for several minutes. The darkness was all-consuming. Warm. Peaceful.

She didn't realize when she drifted off to sleep.

When Heidi awoke, the stars danced above her in mesmerizing loops and spurts. She stared up at them, watching them in wonder. A smile tipped up one of her lips as she moved a hand up to touch the cosmos.

Her hand recoiled when she felt one light touch her finger. Revulsion coiled in her belly, and the muscles in her shoulders tightened.

It took her another full beat for her to realize what happened. She forced a breath in and out. The logical part of her finally won out a moment later.

She didn't see the stars dancing; those didn't move. No, these were lightning bugs. Besides, the canopy overhead was too thick to see the sky during the day. There was no way she could see it at night under the same conditions.

Once she knew what it was, the fear all but disappeared. Still, the physical manifestations of her reaction remained. Her fingers drew little circles at the top of her jawline. She opened and closed her mouth as she urged her body to come down from the sudden fight-or-flight response that overcame her. The rushing of her heart slowed, but only just.

Night fell while she slept, and her fire smoldered instead of burning. How could she let herself be so foolish? She never even built the tent. She was alone. Something could've attacked her in the dark.

From the corner of her eye, a light drew her attention, and Heidi's head whipped around to get a good look at it. Something blue glowed a little deeper into the forest, gliding and dipping like a skillful couple waltzing in a time long since past. She blinked several times to clear her vision, but the blue light remained there, bobbing in the night air expectantly, waiting for her to make the first move.

A part buried deep inside of her screamed at her to stay put, but the magic already held her in its clutches. Without her permission, Heidi's body stood. The light of the luminous figure reflected in her eyes and made them twinkle with similar, complimentary colors.

As her body took step after tentative step forward like a zombie shambling towards its prey, she felt the crushing weight of the magic on her. It held her in its tendrils, wrapping around her in an ever-tightening grip. Try as she might with all of her human senses, she couldn't fight it.

Tears leaked from the corners of her eyes as she walked deeper into the woods. The fire at her campsite was like a long forgotten memory. She knew she'd never be able to backtrack. She was lost, and her remaining hope faded away with each step her body took forward.

As quick as the spell overwhelmed her senses, it released her. Heidi stumbled forward and fell onto her hands and knees. She felt the cold, hard ground beneath her, covered in damp moss and lichen. Her fingers fisted the earth, and she wrenched it up, throwing it wildly in front of her.

As if the pathetic attempt could hurt whatever ensnared her.

Her head dipped, and she sobbed. Few tears came, but those wracking, painful dry sobs rocked her whole body. How could emotions hurt more than physical pain? Nothing she'd experienced before now prepared her for the desolation and emptiness pitted deep inside of her. It ignited as the embers of the tiniest flame and burned hot and fast until ruins were all that remained.

She never should have come here. It was a mistake to leave the safety of her home to recover her long-lost siblings. In her mind's eye, she could see the headlines now: *Schneider Heiress Missing, Search Parties Find Human Remains in Woods, Merchant's Daughter Slain by Her Own Hubris*.

Her body shook; whether the movement came from the cold or as a response to her emotions, she couldn't tell. She doubted much more than base survival instinct remained behind in the depths of her despair.

A strange jingle, like the tinkling of wind chimes, drew her attention. Her head tipped up. Her muscles grew taut, and she prepared to run from whatever predator stalked her in the night. Instead, the sight of a bioluminescent circle of mushrooms greeted her. They glowed in vibrant blues and purples in the otherwise dark woods.

Heidi's heart clenched, and she wondered if the feeling was the beginning of her own death rattles or something else. Did she dare to hope? She knew she stood no chance of survival out here on her own with no supplies. The ring made her feel strangely at ease.

Maybe, she *could* survive.

On her hands and knees, she crawled forward. Damp twigs and leaves dug into her flesh. She winced when she felt them break skin, but she knew she wouldn't live to worry about an infection unless she made it into the circle, her salvation.

Magic overwhelmed her senses the moment her hands and feet entered the illuminated ring of fungi. Night turned to day in an instant before unconsciousness took her.

Before Heidi's eyes opened, she could feel the oppressive heat beating down upon her. If she didn't know any better, she'd think she slept until the hottest day of summer. Either that, or she somehow found herself in the depths of hell. The mere thought of her presence in the bowels of the underworld made her eyes wrench open.

Finding herself propped against the wall of a stone castle, she breathed an instant sigh of relief.

She wasn't dead.

She didn't know where she was, of course, but she wasn't dead. And not dead, was good. She could work with not dead.

"Wow, Heidi. Could you maybe come up with a synonym? Like, alive? Did you hit your head?" she wondered aloud to herself.

Her tongue darted out and licked her lips. Both felt like sandpaper. She woke up just in time. If she stayed here for much longer, she would die of exposure.

She stood on shaking legs. If she could get inside, she'd find some water and maybe get her hands on supplies. Then, she'd find her way back home. After all of this excitement, she gave up. Who cared about her brothers? She already got the best end of the bargain. There were no squabbles or arguments over who would take over the family business when their father retired. Without her brothers around, she won.

She should've thought about this before. Sure, she didn't earn the title fair and square like she would've preferred, but she still got the prize. A pang of regret made her stomach bottom out. If only she would've seen it this way before she ran away. She preferred to avoid pain and heartache if she could help it.

After taking a deep breath, she let herself inside the cavernous fortress.

SIX

HEIDI REGRETTED ENTERING THIS PLACE. Somehow, it grew hotter the deeper she got indoors. Disembodied screams filled the surrounding air, and no matter how hard she tried, she couldn't find the source of the sounds.

After making a dizzying amount of turns she'd never be able to retrace, Heidi found a wide hallway. Her heart skipped a beat. From here, she'd be able to find what she was looking for. At each doorway she stumbled upon, she peeked in to see what awaited her, should she enter. The hall's layout made her zigzag across the way every so often. Several of the rooms she discovered, opened up into dis-interesting, empty rooms. There was a sitting room, bedroom, and a study, but she still found no living beings.

A sense of foreboding overcame her. Despite the cloying heat, she felt a shiver run up her spine. If she looked down, she knew she'd find goosebumps on her arms. Her gut screamed at her to turn back, but she continued to press forward. Besides, how would she get back home from here?

The strange magic yanked her here, and she didn't think she could return outside of a miracle. Somebody here would give her answers. She could feel it.

When she opened a door to discover a blazing inferno on the other side, she let out a little yip of surprise. She stumbled back and covered her mouth with her hands, hoping and praying nobody noticed her.

With the door swung wide open with the force of the heat to propel it, the temperature of the already insufferable hallway skyrocketed. Sweat dripped down the back of her neck as she craned to get a good look inside the oven-like room.

Finally, Heidi heard voices carrying out to her through the portal. She was certain this door opened a gateway to hell, and she needed to leave as soon as possible. Except, a tidbit of conversation caught her attention, and it gave her pause. This was one of those moments where her gut screamed at her to do something while she ignored it. Didn't she used to say something about following her instincts? What happened, and how did she get here?

"What do you *mean* there's an intruder? That's not possible!"

"M- my apologies, my l-l-liege," a skittish voice trailed off, clearly trying to work up the courage to continue speaking. "We detected a magical influx. Security believes a fae felt like playing a prank on an unsuspecting human. We've yet to locate them, but once we do, we'll dispatch them back to the human world."

The walls of the castle shook all around Heidi. Her mind barely registered the words, but her body knew what to do.

She was running before she even heard the creature growl, "Not if I find them first."

Columns in the halls crumbled as she booked it down the too-long corridor. Her heart pounded in her chest. Exerting all her energy to hike yesterday cost her dearly today. Her muscles wailed in protest as she barrelled around a corner she didn't remember taking before.

There *must* be another way out of here. She needed out. Right now. Air came in painful, wheezing pants as she forced herself to keep going top speed for longer. Longer. More. Run harder.

As she urged herself to pick up the pace despite the protest of every muscle and ligament she had, her foot hit the ground wrong. The ball of her ankle twisted, and she tumbled to the ground, landing hard on her hands. She felt her wrist bend back further than it should. A yelp escaped her. Her teeth gnashed together, and her ears strained, trying to hear anything moving towards her.

Heartbeats passed. Seconds wasted. She didn't have time for this! If she couldn't get out of here, she was dead. Her eyes closed, and she pounded on the ground with her fist only to find it caused shooting agony to course up her arm.

When she fell, she thought she hyperextended it, but now, it felt like the equivalent of shoving shards of glass under her skin. Tears sprang to her eyes, and she forced out a breath before gasping another in. Breathing helped control pain, right? If not, every action movie she ever watched lied.

"Don't fail me now, John Wick," she muttered under her breath as she forced herself to her feet. One hand cradled her damaged wrist, holding it against her chest like a delicate vase as she limped forward.

The moment's pause didn't do a thing to slow her racing heart or ease the roll of sweat from her forehead. Each step brought on a fresh wave of anguish as she limped forward at a crawl compared to her earlier sprint. She wasn't ready to die, so she must persevere. Somehow, she would figure out how.

As silently as she could muster, she hobbled forward while tears rolled down her cheeks.

Why? Why her? Some asshole magical creature chose her to play some little game, and now, she'd pay with her life. How was this fair? Life wasn't fair, but she deserved more. She deserved *better*.

An almost imperceptible sound caught her attention, and her head whipped around so fast she felt it crack.

"Ouch!" she whimpered, moving her good hand to rub her neck.

It took her eyes a second to adjust before she spotted something- some*one*- covering their lips with a finger. Were they shushing her? Her first instinct was to tell them off, but given that she wasn't dead at this very moment, she saw the act for what it was: the opportunity for freedom.

Each time she ambled forward, shooting pain made her hop off of her injured foot. If it wouldn't get her killed, or even if it would bring a modicum of relief, she would scream with each step. As it was, all she could do was gasp and grunt under her breath.

It didn't help.

When she made it to the door, she collapsed onto the ground on the other side. The door clicked shut with quiet efficiency. She should feel grateful her rescuer didn't slam the door and draw any more attention, but her focus remained solely on the swelling pain throughout her body. A swell of powerful emotion made her chest tighten, but she fought it. It was not the time for a breakdown. She couldn't afford to lose control. Not right now.

The stranger knelt down and outstretched their hand with their palm facing up. Her ears started ringing. She wondered if the pain, dehydration, or something else caused it, but she couldn't linger on it between her scattering thoughts. The stranger spoke to her, using a low, serious baritone. Their eyes squinted as they spoke, and she was so focused on their expression she didn't process the words until it was too late.

They paused for about two seconds before sniggering, "I have always wanted to say that."

Heidi felt the sudden urge to tell this complete stranger that she hated them. Really? They rescued a young woman from certain death, and they're quoting the Terminator? What happened to bedside manner?

Instead of responding with words, what came out of her mouth was a sort of choked, gawking sound.

"Oh. I forgot. Humans think they're so serious all the time. Let me try something different-"

"No!" she squealed, moving her injured hand to cover their mouth and realizing her mistake much too late. "Please, just get me out of here."

"As you wish," they said, gripping her forearm and whisking her away in a flash of light.

SEVEN

CONSCIOUSNESS RETURNED MUCH slower than it faded out. First, Heidi heard quiet footsteps walking by. Then, she moved and stretched, feeling the softness of sheets rubbing against her skin. Finally, she opened her eyes.

Soft light illuminated the space as it filtered through a window covered in sheer curtains that drifted back and forth with the movements of a light breeze. Whenever the curtain blew away from the window, it gave a breathtaking glimpse of stars twinkling in the twilight sky. She stared for a while as the sight took her breath away.

When she eventually turned her attention back to the room she lie in, it took a minute for her eyes to adjust. It wasn't anything fancy; she discovered. There was only a twin bed, a side table, and an ottoman at the foot of the bed, but it felt like a lived-in and loved home.

For the first time on her rescue minute, a now almost unfamiliar emotion overtook her. It took her a few seconds to come to grips with this strange, warm feeling that filled her from the inside. This place was safe. It felt like the home she left much too long ago and some instinct deep inside of her knew it. The sense of peace here settled over her. She let it embrace her like a warm blanket. Her eyes closed as she enjoyed the overwhelming sensation. She never wanted to leave this place.

Three soft raps on the door startled her. Heidi looked down and pulled the sheet up around her chest. She didn't notice before, but she wore a simple, mint blue set of silk pajamas.

They were sinfully soft. It took an effort to tell herself not to run her hands over the fabric.

"Uh, come in!" she called through the door while trying to calm down and act casual.

The door swung in, and the person who rescued her walked in. Their eyes were icy blue, framed by stark white hair which contrasted honey skin. Their face's soft features complemented angular shoulders.

"Good to see you're awake," they said, leaving the door ajar by a few inches and sitting down on the ottoman. "I hate to put a damper on your time here, but you can't stay in this place much longer. It's taken you a long time to recover."

Heidi's lips pursed. "I couldn't have slept more than a day."

They shook their head. "In a way, you're correct, Heidi. Time moves differently here, but in your world, you've taken several weeks to heal. I'm afraid to make you leave so soon after you've awoken, but we need to get you home before this does any permanent damage."

"How-" she began.

"Do I know your name?" they finished. "To put it in simple terms, magic. If it makes you feel better, you can call me Charlie. The fae sent you here, to a place incompatible with human life. If you dither here too much longer, you'll get stuck."

"Stuck?! What does that mean?"

"To be fixed in a particular position or unable to move or be moved," Charlie deadpanned.

"Did you just define the word stuck?" she asked, sounding equal parts exasperated and impressed.

They bowed from the waist while remaining in their seat. "I live to please. Oh good, good. Thank you for bringing the refreshments, Andromeda. There's little time to waste."

A lovely woman with pale skin placed a silver tray in Heidi's lap. The plate was overladen with food and had a glass of orange juice and a slender vase with a pair of daffodils inside arranged in the upper right of the tray.

Heidi stared at the mountain of food with wide eyes. First, Charlie tried to kick her out the door, and in their next breath, they're asking her to sit down for a quaint brunch?

"I'm confused," she said. "Weren't you just pushing me out of the proverbial nest?"

Charlie smirked. "Consider it a parting gift. Now, get to it. We need to get you out of here within the hour."

They stood up and followed the young woman who brought the food out the door. "Thank you, Andi. Let's check in on how Orion's fared with his task."

She stared after the odd pair, pondering the strange encounter for too long before digging into her meal. The meal was chock full of protein, including beans, eggs, sausage, and a T-bone steak. Each bite tasted more delicious than the last, and by the time she finished eating, there was nothing but bones left on her plate.

Heidi sat there, rubbing her stomach with satisfaction. She didn't think she could eat so much, but she managed it somehow. The door to her room opened, and she turned her head to find a burly man entering the room. His dyed hair matched the piercing bright blue color of his eyes.

"You're finished. Good," he said, placing a familiar, overfilled bag on the floor beside the door. The thing looked like it weighed nothing to him. "Charlie asked me to give this to you so you could put something comfortable on before you set off. I'll leave you to it, but don't take too long."

When the door shut behind him, she slipped out of bed, rubbing her temples with the fingers of her left hand. As she stood, she expected to feel dizzy or otherwise unwell, but she realized she felt better than ever instead. Her head didn't hurt. All her aches and pains from hiking were long gone, and even her broken fingernails and little imperfections like the scar on the back of her hand from the time she cut herself on a loose furniture staple had disappeared. Yet, the lingering sting in her pinkie from the witch using her blood for that spell remained. She didn't know what this place was, but no doubts remained in her mind after seeing all the little changes: it was magic, pure and simple.

She wouldn't think too hard on what type of magic could cure all her minor aches, pains, cuts, and scrapes while leaving one nagging issue to fester. It piqued her curiosity, but she sensed a danger in exploring all avenues of thought as well. A foreboding shadow hovered over her in this place. That's when she realized it; Charlie was right. She needed to get out of here.

Despite shaking hands and stumbling feet, Heidi got ready in no time. As she finished, she tossed her miraculously retrieved backpack over her shoulder and wrenched the door open. She didn't know why, but she expected to find the space on the other side larger than life somehow, be it from magic or other means.

It was just a hallway, and beside her room, Charlie leaned against the wall with arms crossed over their chest.

"Let's roll."

"Please stop quoting movies."

"First, the last one wasn't a movie. Second, you wound me, darling," Charlie said, putting on a pair of sunglasses and motioning for her to follow.

Heidi kept pace. She followed close behind the kind stranger, determined to get out of here safely. It felt strange to be so close with somebody she met less than an hour ago to her reckoning, but something about Charlie felt disarming. Maybe wisdom wasn't her strong suit, but some instinct told her to do as they said. She hoped her gut kept her alive once again.

They left the building, a tall woman with sharp facial features and unwieldy red hair held the door open for them.

"Thanks, Polly," Charlie said cordially as they walked by and down a well-worn path through intimidatingly tall conifers. As they continued on, the weather grew colder and darker.

Heidi crossed her hands over her chest and rubbed her arms to keep warm as puffs of warm breath became visible in the air. She couldn't see too far ahead, so she kept her eyes glued to the trail. At least, she could see that still.

Charlie glanced over their shoulder at her.

"Oh, rats. How could I forget?" they asked, coming to a stop.

She stared at Charlie for a minute. People didn't talk like them anymore, and she wondered where they came from or how they got here. It scared her to think about how old Charlie was. Ignorance was bliss. She wanted it to stay that way.

Before she could voice her questions, they said, "Wait here just a tick. I forgot something."

"But-" she said.

Charlie was gone before she even blinked.

Heidi stood there, aimless. All she knew was she needed out of this place as soon as possible, and her wayfinder told her to take a break.

Her fingers rubbed her temples. She inhaled and released a heavy breath. Calmer minds prevailed. A few more minutes wouldn't hurt. Besides, it sounded like Charlie forgot something important. She could only hope they didn't abandon her during her escape for something frivolous.

For a split second, her mind summoned the strange being walking back with a pair of popsicles for them to enjoy together. She shook her head. They better not, or she'd give them a piece of her mind for wasting her time.

EIGHT

WITH EACH PASSING HEARTBEAT, IT FELT like a weight grew in Heidi's chest. Her muscles coiled tighter, and her eyes darted back and forth, searching for an imaginary assailant crouched behind the trunk of a tree. Each breath became quicker, more shallow.

She let the arms of her overladen backpack slide off. It hit the ground with a heavy thump.

Without the weight holding her down, she felt safer. Her father would say she was ready for anything, even an attacker coming out of the woods. She kept her head on a swivel. Still, she saw nothing. No movement. She heard nothing, not even wildlife in the forest. The lack of noise unsettled her further.

A couple more heartbeats passed before a low, droning sound coming from a distance drew her attention. Her stomach lurched, and she took a step backward off of the trail as the noise grew into a cacophony.

It took her too long to recognize the commotion as some sort of motor, but before she could think about it too hard, Charlie pulled to a stop in front of her.

"Is that a snowmobile?" she asked, mouth agape.

"Careful with that expression. You'll catch flies," they said, extending a finger and gently nudging her chin up to close her mouth.

Charlie hopped off the vehicle and removed a backpack. Reaching inside, they pulled out a puffy jacket with a hood, followed by a pair of ski pants.

"Throw these on."

Heidi didn't think twice. She yanked the jacket out of Charlie's hands and pulled it around her, zipping and snapping it shut. The ski pants took a little longer now that she had the cumbersome jacket on, and she wondered if they gave them to her in this order just to watch her struggle. Once she finished, she looked up at them.

"Thank you for everything."

They shook their head back and forth, tutting. "I'm not done yet, darling."

"Oh-kay," she drawled.

They pulled the bone from the T-bone steak she ate with breakfast out of the bag.

"You almost forgot this."

"Uh, thanks?"

She didn't mean for it to sound rude, but it still came out as an insensitive question. Why was this important in any way? It took her several seconds to realize the bone no longer had remnants of meat on it. In fact, it looked immaculate. How could anybody get it so clean in such a short amount of time?

Yet again, Charlie left her with more questions than answers.

"You've heard of skeleton keys, yes? Turns out the myth is more true than you think. It's a one-time use, though. So, choose your door wisely."

Charlie grabbed her backpack and shoved the bone into one of the outer pouches. They tightened a bungee cord around it with its plastic drawstring.

"Consider this a gift from my siblings and I as an apology for our dickhead of a cousin. Sonny's job stresses him out, and he takes it out on people."

Heidi gulped audibly. "I'm glad you're not like him," she said with a shiver running up her spine.

They lowered their sunglasses. "I need you to listen carefully, now. Are you paying attention?"

She nodded several times, shuffling her feet as she drew closer to hear Charlie better.

They glanced at a watch, and when they started speaking, they spoke faster than normal. "I did my best to keep you safe while considering this plan, but timing is key. In one minute, I want you to take the snowmobile and go down this hill as fast as it'll take you. Follow the path. Do not deviate. When you get to the end, you'll find an open portal. It will bring you back to your world. The further you go, the colder it will get. This is normal, just keep going. If you hear anything, don't stop. Follow the plan until you get home."

"I know you have questions, and I don't have time to answer. I have a few pieces of advice for you before you go. Be careful with your use of language, especially words of gratitude. Fae love exploiting lazy expressions. Fifteen seconds."

They stepped forward to help her onto the snowmobile. "The throttle's that one," they said, pointing. "Don't believe everything you see and hear. There are many illusions within and without this world. Good luck, Heidi."

Charlie cleared away and shouted, "Go!"

She flew forward into the frigid air ahead.

Heidi never rode a snowmobile before. Extreme sports were usually not in her wheelhouse, but desperate times called for a little improvisation. Thankfully, steering the thing came to her easily enough, and Charlie pointed out the throttle, which was its own blessing. Her fingers gripped it tight. She was determined to go as fast as possible and make it to the end of the road without incident.

Her unexpectedly kind host didn't tell her what awaited her here, but from context clues, she didn't want to find out either. The icy air stung her eyes, making her wish for a pair of sunglasses or goggles to shield them from the elements. If she got out of here, she was sure she'd find ice crystals permanently stuck to her eyelashes.

The idea made a shiver run up her spine, but she wasn't sure the feeling came from the cold.

Even though she couldn't see it, she could feel something out there. Could it see her? Was it watching her? Something felt off. Whatever sixth sense humans had kept her on high alert as the vehicle flew forward, gliding over the snow. Sight meant nothing when magic became involved. Reason told her everything she needed to know.

An enemy awaited her somewhere out there, and if it found her, she'd be dead.

The thought made her heart skip a beat. She vowed to herself these wouldn't be her last.

Finally, her eyes spotted a break in the trees. A smirk drew at her lips. The end of this adventure was near, and she wanted to go home. But as she got closer and closer to the tree line, the harder it was to see the path. The path! Didn't Charlie tell her to follow the path? She mustn't deviate. Her life depended on it. Her head swiveled, but there was nothing to be seen. Did Charlie lie? How could she be such a fool?

"Dammit," she said under her breath. She couldn't hear herself over the sound of the motor, and speaking to herself was no comfort this time.

As she broke through the trees and into the snow covered clearing beyond, her eyes caught sight of a massive form with red, glowing eyes. She did a double take, and it took her several seconds too long to realize her distraction kept her from holding the throttle all the way down. Her fingers squeezed tight, and the snowmobile lurched forward once again over a small hill. She got some air before hitting the ground harder than she expected. It made her lose her grip again.

A squeal of terror escaped her as she started going full throttle again. The vehicle jerked forward again. What happened to its former speed? Did her distraction mean this was the end?

No. No, she wouldn't let it. She hunkered down close against the vehicle, trying to keep herself out of the elements. If she lost grip again, she'd never make it out of here.

Her heart pounded hard in her chest while she searched for her way out. An exit must exist. She just needed to find it. Of all the people she met along the way, she trusted Charlie. Charlie wouldn't lead her astray.

Some part of her spotted a break in the trees before she processed it. The snowmobile zoomed toward her salvation as she prayed to make it without getting caught.

The whole world rumbled beneath and around her. It sounded like a cat jumped on all the wrong keys at the bass end of a piano. The hairs on the back of her neck stood on end while the snow shifted like quicksand in a horror movie around her.

One of the vehicle tracks hit something solid and hard.

Heidi didn't have enough time to react before the world turned itself on its head. Somebody screamed. It took her too long to realize the sound ripped itself out of her throat. The world turned from white to black.

Then, she blinked. Despite the chill, her body felt warm, or was it the blood dripping down her face?

Even though she wanted to lie there and wait for help to come, she pushed herself up. Beside her, the snowmobile's motor hummed, much too close for comfort. Her luck, or lack thereof, astounded her sometimes. With ringing ears, she stumbled to her feet. It felt like she was trying to wade through chest deep water.

A heartless, female voice crooned from somewhere behind her, "I can smell you. Your warm blood calls to me, sweet and delicious."

The voice dragged out the 's' for several seconds. It made Heidi's skin crawl, like serpents slithering just beneath the surface. The hairs on the back of her neck prickled, standing on end as she scrambled forward. The momentum of her fall threw her closer to the portal. She couldn't see it before. Now, it shone clear as day. The familiar light and warmth of the sun radiated with the inviting energy of hearth and home.

Home. A pang of guilt thrummed in her chest.

Once she finished this blasted errand, she could return to her family, and she never wanted to leave again. Maybe she'd become an eccentric shut-in obsessed with the care and collection of cats. Yes, that was it. She'd become a crazy cat lady. She needed to get out of here so she could use her father's wealth and stature in their community to open a cat rescue. No, better, a cat café. That's it. The cats needed her.

Each footstep felt like the effort she imagined carrying another person over her shoulder would take, and the vile voice kept taunting her as it drew closer, louder.

"I can already taste it. Your fear is like the most delicious spice. Such nuance, so robust." Again, the 's' dragged on, and the woman popped the 't.'

Heidi jumped, and her feet shuffled in the snow, causing a shooting pain to run up her leg.

Why didn't shock keep her from feeling this? She couldn't afford to waver. Death wasn't an option.

"I'm not ready to die," she said her thoughts aloud.

"Legends never die, my sweet. Can you imagine them telling the tale of you meeting the sun and stars?" the woman said, pausing for several heart-pounding seconds. "And then, the moon goddess herself devoured the heroine of our tale."

A low chuckle rumbled the ground beneath her, and she almost lost her footing again. She could feel a breath-like wind coming from behind her. Flakes of snow rushed forward, and so did Heidi.

She could count the strides it would take to get to the portal. Five. It wasn't too many steps. Her body could make it that far, at least.

Four. Maybe bigger steps would get her out faster.

The third step made her stumble. The snow and ice started melting here. Was it because of the cruel god behind her, her own warmth, or the portal? She didn't know, and she had little time to ponder it. Her feet must keep moving.

Two. She could feel glacial talons too-close at hand. The edges of the portal she spotted a few moments earlier were tapering off. Didn't Charlie tell her it would close soon?

She threw herself forward. If she didn't make it through, she was dead either way.

Her last thought before the pain and blood loss overwhelmed her was, 'One.' She was the only sister of seven useless brothers who did nothing for her. Why was she the one trying to save them again?

NINE

PAIN. FIRST, HEIDI REGISTERED ACHES and pains all over her body, but this agony meant something important. The anguish her body felt meant she was alive. She didn't expect to live.

Instead, she thought she'd be dead with her soul languishing in the belly of the moon goddess by now. She wondered if she should feel grateful about making it out, or if more fear and torment loomed overhead. Why couldn't this be easy? Everything else came to her so readily, but ever since leaving home, things kept going wrong.

It made her wonder if her parents handed the world to her on a silver platter out of grief. Did they give up on her brothers and accept her as some sort of meager consolation prize? Is this why nothing went her way since leaving?

A wave of foreign emotion hit her like a truck. It hurt physically as much as emotionally. She recognized parts of it: rage, betrayal, sorrow, embarrassment. It came so unexpectedly that she didn't have the faculties to register and process it all.

In the next moment, she was on her feet, marching towards the god forsaken castle on the mountain. She would finish this. She owed it to herself to see the truth for herself. When her brothers returned home, she planned to prove to her parents that their daughter deserved to inherit the family business.

Every part of her body screamed at her to rest and ease the pain, begging her to stop and give up on her mission. Instead, she ignored her body's protests and pressed on.

By the time Heidi made it to the castle door, she was panting. One of her hands clutched onto a stitch in her side. She leaned against the wall and closed her eyes.

"You can do this, Heidi," she said through gritted teeth. Everything hurt, but she came all this way. "It's time to finish this. Just grab the stupid bone key, go inside, and release the spell. Easy peasy lemon squeezy."

Her eyes flew wide open. A jolt shook her to her very core, and this time, it wasn't pain talking. "Nevermind, it's stressy depressy lemon zesty."

She shook with a dry sob, too dehydrated to produce tears anymore. Where the fuck was her backpack? Charlie packed the key in there for her. It took her several seconds to retrace her steps mentally. When she woke up, she didn't remember seeing her bag. It must've fallen off of her when she crashed the snowmobile.

Every curse she knew flooded her mind, and a few escaped her lips as well. How in the world could she make it inside now? Nobody answered the door when she knocked, and the skeleton key Charlie gave her was gone. With no T-bone steaks for miles, she didn't know what to do. Hunting was out of the question. Since she didn't know what she was doing, she'd likely hurt herself rather than whatever animal she attempted to kill.

What choices did this leave her?

Heidi groaned. The sound echoed around her, like the moans and wails of tortured souls in the underworld. It sounded strangely satisfying. This place felt like her own personal hell. Now, it sounded the way she imagined it should.

As far as she could tell, her options were to give up and leave or to find a bone some other way. A shiver ran up her spine, and it wasn't from the cold. She would never get used to that feeling of chilling eeriness.

The foreboding feeling shifted, and she found it strange how the intangible weight of decision and expectation could make a physical object feel heavier. As soon as she considered the merit of finding another bone, the knife she brought with her grew heavier in her pocket. It never felt like this before, but the thing felt somehow heftier now.

After everything she'd gone through, she couldn't imagine giving up now that she'd gotten so close to the end. Her prize was in sight. She just needed to get inside and figure out how to lift her brothers' curse. That's all. The worst of this nightmare was behind her, she'd left it back in the other world with the moon and sun.

Only one last step, one ultimate sacrifice, stood in her way.

She looked down at her hands. Her eyes lingered on her fingers. Searching. Thinking.

Her hands balled into fists. She opened and closed them. Resolve settled somewhere deep inside of her. Her shoulders grew tense. She knew what she needed to do, but she wasn't sure if she had the strength to go through with it.

Once again, her eyes closed, but this time, she prayed. She didn't know where she was when she met Charlie, but she knew one thing with certainty. Charlie saved her from a fate worse than death. If the moon goddess caught her, Heidi doubted her death would've been fast. No, the goddess was cruel, and so was the other one. She remembered the burning heat and her lightheadedness. Without Charlie, she wouldn't be here, so she prayed to Charlie in thanks, hoping to request one last favor.

When she finished, she sat on the ground and crossed her legs. Her back leaned against the wall while her hands worked. She ripped the hem off of the bottom of her shirt. Good thing it was long. The image of meeting her brothers for the first time while wearing a midriff made her face screw up in distaste.

Once she had enough fabric in hand, she wrapped it tight around her left wrist, doing her best to restrict circulation. She elevated her arm and hand to help. Then, with her right hand, she grabbed the knife. She wished she had some rubbing alcohol or something in order to sterilize it. The logical part of her knew she stood a good chance of introducing an infection even if she somehow kept herself from bleeding out.

"Don't psych yourself out, Heidi," she said.

She wondered when she started seeking the comfort of talking to herself during all of this, but she shook her head. The time for distractions passed long ago.

"Stop distracting yourself. Either do it or leave, you silly girl."

She locked her jaw and gritted her teeth. Part of her wished for something to bite down onto.

The edge of her blade pressed into her flesh. At the bottom joint of her pinky, it took little effort. Didn't she see an internet post about fingers being as difficult to remove as biting into a carrot?

Her scream echoed in the mountains.

TEN

TEARS STRUCK THE DIRT ALONGSIDE blood splatter. It looked like a Rorschach inkblot, but much more macabre. And much more painful. She preferred figuring out the 'correct' answers to those psychological tests over this torment.

Heidi's breathing came in shuddering gasps. A near-constant whimper escaped her, but she forced her body up. She'd come too far to admit defeat. Besides, she tried to think on the bright side; the pinky she pricked for Caysi's spell couldn't bother her if it didn't exist.

Now that the deed was done, she needed to get inside so she could clean up her wound somehow. She kept her left hand elevated over her heart while she used her other to grab the damned key. The flesh on the bone was still warm. Blood covered her arm, shirt, and finger. The hot, slickness made her gut churn. Soon, it would coagulate, which brought on another fresh wave of sickness at the mere thought of the sensory input.

Holding her breath, she kept herself from puking as she shoved the key into the door and twisted. The lock clicked, and the door swung open, allowing her entrance into the mountain.

As she stepped inside, she expected to find old-timey torches to light her path. Instead, LED chandeliers hung in the vaulted ceiling above her. They looked tacky amongst the majesty of the rest of the castle, but she didn't live here. Why did she care?

She walked down a corridor that felt entirely too long. Was some sort of magic or uncanny valley effect confusing her, or was it blood loss? She grimaced at her finger stub, forcing herself to look away. There was no time to worry; it was time for action.

A sigh of relief escaped her when she found a massive great room with room for comfortable seating by a fire and a twelve-person table set for a service of seven on the other side of the room. Colored glass fixtures, white fabrics, and orange-colored wooden chairs, which reminded her of Halloween decorated the room.

She felt tempted to yell trick-or-treat.

"Well, that's inappropriate," she muttered to herself.

With sweat beading on her forehead, she stumbled over to the fire. The large, plush armchairs called to her, and when she fell into the one closest to the hearth, she sank into it with a moan of appreciation. She missed the comforts of home.

With a start, she realized she moved her wrist below her heart, and she elevated it again. How could she already feel the thing swelling after a few seconds? Her eyes lingered on the fireplace poker. Knowing she needed to cauterize her wound and wanting to do it were two different things. She gulped as she grabbed the handle and shoved the tip into the flames.

As the tip of the metal began to glow with the heat, her heart picked up its pace. More fear trying to control her. She wouldn't let it. She was the master of her fate.

When the fire made the metal bright white, she pulled it out of the flame. Even with her good hand, the heaviness surprised her.

Occasional pulses of blood poured over her hand. She needed to stop the bleeding soon, even if she wouldn't bleed out right away.

With great difficulty, she propped the poker up so that it would fall away from her if she passed out. She got lucky with the amputation, but burning a wound shut? She doubted she'd get so lucky.

Her hand shook as she moved it toward the poker. It felt warmer with each inch forward. Dread filled her. This would *not* be fun.

"You can do this, Heidi. You already went through hell and came back. What's a bit more pain? Alright. We're going in one, two, three."

After her little pep talk, she thrust her hand forward, pressing the open wound onto the inferno-like steel.

The screams echoing throughout the castle sounded like a banshee. They wrenched from her throat of their own accord. After several drawn out moments, the yell became deep coughs until she coughed up blood.

The red-hot poker fell away, clattering to the stone floor, and the girl fell backward into the plush armchair, unconscious.

By the time Heidi awoke, the smell of food permeated the great room. She couldn't distinguish the individual scents brought to the table, but she could tell it was hearty and flavorful. It felt like a strength workout just to open her eyes, but at least, they opened. She could've died.

Instead, she lived another day. A rush of gratitude overcame her. Once she got out of here, she would go home to big hugs from her mother and father. They'd scold her, but she knew they'd feel so relieved by her return that they wouldn't mean it. One of her lips curled up at the idea. She couldn't decide if she missed them, her bed, or a home-cooked meal more. She wanted to go home sooner rather than later.

She turned her head to look at the dining table. While she was unconscious, somebody set the table for service of eight. At each place setting, a glass of red wine waited. She remained the sole guest despite all the fanfare.

Rude. How could anybody allow such a delicious smelling meal to go to waste?

Right on cue, her stomach rumbled with gnawing hunger. She wondered when she last ate, remembering Charlie delivered her the steak breakfast most recently. It felt like a lifetime ago.

She stood up in a rush and regretted it when her head spun. She should've expected it, but she held onto the couch for support and waited for the feeling to pass instead.

Her eyes set themselves on the table with determination. She planned to devour every morsel on the table until nothing remained besides scraps.

She sat in front of the first place setting and realized her brain severely overestimated her hunger. Her eyes grew to the size of saucers. There was no way she could eat every single meal, so instead, she chose to eat a little at each plate. She didn't know what possessed her to do so. Maybe she felt a little more chaotic today, or it was a symptom of blood loss and shock?

Regardless, instead of eating at the single place setting made for her, she ate a few morsels at each seat, ending with her own. When she got to her place, she felt so thirsty that she drank her entire glass of wine.

After placing the cup back down, she leaned back in her seat, full and sated. One of her hands rubbed her overstuffed belly. It felt like her first meal after several days, but there was no way more than a few hours could've passed during her little nap.

A seed of doubt wriggled its way into her mind. Didn't she also pass out after escaping the moon? A chill running up her spine forced her to sit up straighter. How long was she unconscious? And on second thought, there were no clocks in this room. It stood to reason she could have slept for a longer period here as well.

An unexpected sound cut Heidi's thoughts short. At first, she couldn't put her finger on what she heard. A few seconds passed before she processed the noise.

Wings.

She could hear the flapping beat of wings growing more distinct in the air above her. Her heart rate picked up. She wasn't ready to meet her brothers yet. After all the pain and grief she'd gone through, she wanted to know she found the right birds.

Thinking fast, she slipped the stolen signet ring from her right thumb and set it inside her emptied glass. It clinked in the bottom before growing still. Then, she ducked under the table, ignoring her aching limbs and over-full belly.

A memory sparked as she lie in wait under the table. She remembered being a small child and hiding from her parents under the dinner table. Back then, she paid little attention to the hushed conversations shared between their staff, but on that afternoon, she overheard Greta speaking with someone about 'the young master.' Back then, she thought the woman meant Christoph, her father, but couldn't the words mean someone else entirely? Like one of her brothers?

Rage coiled deep in her gut. Did Greta purposely cause all of this, or was she just a shameless gossip? Now that her father sacked the woman, she doubted she'd get an answer. To think her family trusted the servant once.

Heidi punched the stone floor with a fist. She flexed her hand and shook it. Tingles rushed down her fingers and up her wrist. What a bonehead move. Why would she punch a solid object? She didn't need to hurt herself right now. In fact, that was the last thing she needed to do. Still, it felt good to release some of those repressed emotions. When she got back home, she needed to find a constructive way to let them out while proving herself as the best of the Schneider siblings.

The beating wings grew louder. *Closer*. The black linen tablecloth waved with the force. As the sounds quieted, the flutter of the fabric slowed down again.

One of Heidi's hands covered her mouth to keep her from drawing attention to herself. Unfamiliar voices arose from the otherworldly silence above her.

A little jolt of hope lightened her spirit. Yes! For the first time, it felt like she was coming to the end of a long journey. She came all this way, faced so many obstacles, and she made it. Today, she met her brothers and brought them home.

She could see the headlines now: *Heidi Schneider deemed a hero by the town for single-handedly returning her brothers home after sixteen years*. Her pride swelled. She basked in the feeling for a moment. *This*. This was why she overcame all those hardships.

ELEVEN

A DEEP VOICE SPOKE FROM THE HEAD OF the table. It sounded familiar, like her father, but she knew it couldn't be him. This *must* be one of her brothers. Yet, the familiarity ended with the tones and speech patterns it spoke in. The voice gurgled and croaked. It sounded like it took great effort to create the syllables. The raven formed the words with the slow deliberateness of practiced speech.

"Another unproductive day."

"It's not every day we can help people cursed like us," a second, equally haunting voice grated.

"I hope not. Nobody deserves to live a cursed life, and we can't all be like the first. He prefers this form."

Heidi could hear differences in tone and inflection, but she couldn't quite put her finger on who was talking from her place. She wondered if they'd speak more if using a beak to talk weren't so difficult. That was a question for another time. The plates tinkled and clattered as beaks stole food away one morsel at a time. For a moment, she realized these sounds might've been the familiar sounds of home in another life, except for the eeriness with which ravens spoke like humans.

A wave of sadness washed over her, making goosebumps come up all over her arms. The meal in her stomach wasn't sitting so well anymore. She didn't know what caused her brothers to transform into the beasts they were, but she knew she missed out on something special because of it. Perhaps, it should make her angry instead, though there was little use in allowing her rage and resentment over the loss to take control. She said a silent prayer to mourn the loss of a childhood filled with love and joy. Of course, her parents were wonderful, but they couldn't give her the companionship and support of a sibling.

"Oi, Claus! Did you steal my potatoes? Cough them back up, those are mine. Why do we do this every day, you jerk?"

"I took them because you ate my bratwurst, Anton. Stop accusing me of being a thief when you started it."

"Come to think of it, I'm missing my veggies," a third voice chimed in.

A quiet settled over the room in stark contrast to the din from before.

"Why is the table set for eight today?" the first voice asked. "Were we expecting company?"

"Not that I can remember, Friedrich."

Heidi tensed beneath the table. She held her breath and covered her mouth with a hand. If the ravens were as awful as the gods she met on her journey, she would sneak out when night fell and never look back at this place again, but if they were her brothers, they'd recognize her little trap.

Then, she'd bring them home.

A pregnant pause fell over the table for several seconds. A pair of wings flapped, becoming closer and louder. Heidi ducked lower under the table, as if her mere presence near one raven would alert the rest to her location.

"There's something at the bottom," Friedrich said.

The wine glass she emptied chimed. A beak must've bumped against it. "Damned this useless appendage."

The glass clattered down and bumped into something, probably a plate, from the sounds of it. The tablecloth shifted with the movement, and Heidi flinched.

If this was the witch's idea of a terrible trick, she couldn't afford to fall into the woman's trap. So much time had passed since she shared the cup of tea with Caysi. It felt like years when it was probably less than a week. Part of her still reeled at the fact that she promised the witch her firstborn whenever, or if ever, that happened. When she got around to dating, that would be an interesting conversation to have.

"There was a signet ring inside the glass. This is our crest, the Schneider crest. Who could've done this?" Friedrich said, practically demanding answers from his clueless avian siblings.

"Well, it can't be mum or dad's. They would've come here by now if they wanted us back," Anton responded first.

The world stood still as they each pondered the ramifications of their discovery.

"I hope it's our sister," one of them said. "She's the key to breaking our curse, isn't she?"

"You can't know that, Bruno."

"Am I the only one around here with a shred of hope left? You're right, I don't know, but this can't be all that's left of our lives."

Voices rang out in chorus, getting louder and louder as they tried in vain to speak over each other. The clatter of utensils and flutter of wings grew with each passing second, and soon, scraps of food landed on the floor beside the table.

Heidi's eyes darted to the side, watching in horror as the kerfuffle played out above her. The hand she used to cover her mouth turned into a fist. Were these dunderheads fighting over something as simple as one of them daring to hope for a rescue? Her heart pounded in her chest as she tried to calm herself down, but with each new scrap of food that hit the ground, she knew discovery grew closer. It was only a matter of time before a raven hit the floor.

She needed to decide what to do. They recognized her signet, so at least, she found the right ravens. But after hearing their petty squabbling, did they deserve a rescue? Now that she stood at the end of the tracks she set for herself, she feared taking the last step and making a mistake in her haste. She just hoped that a simple mistake wouldn't make the choice for her. Like her father. When they discussed the events leading to her brothers' disappearance, she knew from his body language how much he regretted his words all those years ago. She didn't want to become the next Schneider to regret their actions. Her eyes closed, and she tried to predict the future to the best of her abilities, thinking about each choice and its ramifications.

If she waited out the argument and the darkness of nightfall, she'd be home in a few days. Her parents would welcome her with open arms, but she'd get punished after the relief wore off. They'd name her the sole heir to the family name and fortune. A good life filled with unknown joy awaited her, but two thoughts loomed at the back of her mind.

She'd always ask herself one question. 'What if.' What if she saved her brothers? Without saving them, she would never know. On the other hand, she could reveal herself now. Hopefully, the transformed Schneider brothers would recognize her as their salvation. Blood or family magic of some sort would end their curse. Otherwise, they'd find some other way to break the decade-old spell. They'd go home, and her parents would be grateful.

Then, the real challenge began. She planned to use everything she'd learned to prove beyond any doubt that she was the best and deserved to be named heir. It's what she set out for at the beginning. She didn't want the consolation prize. When she won, she'd get the satisfaction of knowing she earned the accolades rather than getting the handout.

"*Don't believe everything you see and hear*," Charlie's words echoed in her mind.

What choice should she make? What choice did she even have?

A soft thump on the stone floor made her head jerk to the side so quickly she felt the whiplash. Her eyes went wide as the room fell silent. Heartbeats passed in stunned silence until the raven hopped up to its feet.

"Oi! You didn't have to knock me down, you dirty little-" the bird hesitated. One black, beady eye settled itself on Heidi hidden beneath the table. "Of all the ridiculous hiding places. Did you think under the dining table was a good idea, Heidi?"

The hairs on the back of her neck stood on end. Didn't her parents tell her she didn't have a name for about a week after she was born? It made sense to her since even the doctors didn't know she would survive for long. So how did this bird know her name? The ramifications made her blood go cold. Her mind and body wasted their time concentrating on the fear, freezing when she should've run away.

Reality struck her before she mustered the strength in her aching body to move. Somehow, some way, she fell for a trap. How could she be so blind? She walked right into their hands. Her breath hitched and her nine fingers tingled. The room spun as she scrambled out from under the table to run.

In her haste, her head hit the edge of the wood. Her vision turned red as she felt warmth rush from her scalp. Heidi toppled forward into an unconscious heap.

Friedrich looked at the battered-looking teen with a cool gaze. He shifted from one foot to the other, the only sign of any hesitation or internal conflict before he said, "Well, boys. You know what the witch told us to do."

A single caw echoed throughout the great room before the seven sprung into action, flying towards the body on the floor. Each of the Schneider brothers took their turns eating morsel by morsel.

EPILOGUE

AN ALMOST THIRTY-YEAR-OLD MAN stood beside a reporter. A lock of long, cropped dirty-blond hair fell into one eye, and he flicked it out of the way with a twist of his head. His brown eyes and neutral expression were attentive to the woman even though his impatience was getting the better of him. He could do without the spotlight in the wake of everything that happened, but their family's notoriety demanded attention. The public needed to see some sort of resolution in the face of this mess. He hoped they'd be through with the last of the questions before long.

"How did you and the other Schneider brothers break the raven curse after so long?"

"With the help of the town witch, Caysi. She cast a spell to help us break it."

"Can you tell us anything about the ongoing search for your little sister, Heidi?" the reporter asked in a clinical tone.

"Not much to update, I'm afraid. From what we were told, she went missing a couple weeks before the curse broke. We've spent most of our time since then trying to catch up on everything we missed after our transformation," the eldest brother, Friedrich, said. "It's a shame. I would've liked to get to know her. I hope the authorities will find her and bring her home soon."

"Is there anything you're most looking forward to now that you're back?"

He hesitated for a moment. "I'm looking forward to learning the family business. I missed out on quite a few life lessons with my father. There's a lot of catching up to do."

The woman smiled and nodded. "I bet there is. Well, before we wrap up, is there anything else you'd like to share?"

"I just wanted to say thank you. We've received an outpouring of love and support ever since we returned, and our family is forever grateful for everyone's kind words."

"Thanks for your time today, mister Schneider. This is Mila, signing off with channel seven news."

"Cut," the cameraman said. He stepped forward and offered a hand to Friedrich. "It was a pleasure to meet you, and welcome back."

"Appreciate it. Have a safe trip." He stepped inside and watched from the window as the news crew packed up and drove off. He felt somebody walk up behind him, but they didn't speak right away, formulating their words.

"Should we tell them? They deserve to know about her," Bruno said.

"You're too soft. It's already done. What difference will incriminating ourselves make? Take the witch's gift and leave well enough alone."

"But-"

"No buts. We got our lives back, use it wisely. The witch isn't our problem anymore. Somebody else can deal with her or learn the hard way."

Bruno glared at his brother. If looks could kill, the other man would be dead. "Fine, have it your way. Like always, golden boy. I'll be the one saying I told you so when she hurts someone else."

Friedrich didn't bother responding. Instead, he went back to staring out the window. One of his hands moved up to his jaw and massaged. It took all his mental faculties to keep himself from cawing during the interview. He knew they had a long road to recovery ahead of them. Like he said, the witch was the least of their worries.

THE END

JOIN THE CAWS

Forgive my pun, but if you enjoyed this book, please consider taking a few moments to share your feelings about this twisted fairy tale retelling on your favorite book review site or at the retailer where you bought this novella.

CAN'T WAIT FOR MORE?

Subscribe to my mailing list for updates when new books become available.

Subscribepage.io/uPXPSm

ABOUT THE AUTHOR

I'm a semi-professional, semi-crazed author who lives off of caffeine and spite. My pen names are Maria Caiazza and M. W. McLeod. If you love exploring the line between what makes a hero or a villain and reading about characters you're not sure you can agree with, you're in the right place. Home of modern fairy tale retellings with a dark twist and much more coming soon.

www.ingramcontent.com/pod-product-compliance
Lightning Source LLC
Chambersburg PA
CBHW020524310726
48979CB00014B/2199/J

9781957257150